WRITTEN BY
JULIA DONALDSON

ILLUSTRATED BY
AXEL SCHEFFLER

THE GRUFFALO'S CHILD

MACMILLAN CHILDREN'S BOOKS

The Gruffalo said that no gruffalo should
Ever set foot in the deep dark wood.
"Why not? Why not?" *"Because if you do*
The Big Bad Mouse will be after you.
I met him once," said the Gruffalo.
"I met him a long long time ago."

"What does he look like? Tell us, Dad.
Is he terribly big and terribly bad?"

For Franzeska – J.D.
For Freya and Cora – A.S.

First published 2004 by Macmillan Children's Books
This edition published 2019 by Macmillan Children's Books
an imprint of Pan Macmillan
20 New Wharf Road, London N1 9RR
Associated companies throughout the world
www.panmacmillan.com

ISBN 978-1-5098-9447-5

1 3 5 7 9 8 6 4 2

A CIP catalogue record for this book is available
from the British Library.

Printed in China

"I can't quite remember," the Gruffalo said.
Then he thought for a minute and scratched his head.

"The Big Bad Mouse is terribly strong
And his scaly tail is terribly long.

His eyes are like pools of terrible fire
And his terrible whiskers are tougher than wire."

One snowy night when the Gruffalo snored
The Gruffalo's Child was feeling bored.

The Gruffalo's Child was feeling brave
So she tiptoed out of the gruffalo cave.
The snow fell fast and the wind blew wild.
Into the wood went the Gruffalo's Child.

Aha! Oho! A trail in the snow!
Whose is this trail and where does it go?
A tail poked out of a logpile house.
Could this be the tail of the Big Bad Mouse?

Out slid the creature. His eyes were small
And he didn't have whiskers – no, none at all.

"You're not the Mouse." *"Not I,"* said the snake.
"He's down by the lake – eating gruffalo cake."

The snow fell fast and the wind blew wild.
"I'm not scared," said the Gruffalo's Child.

Aha! Oho! Marks in the snow!

Whose are these claw marks? Where do they go?

Two eyes gleamed out of a treetop house.

Could these be the eyes of the Big Bad Mouse?

Down flew the creature. His tail was short
And he didn't have whiskers of any sort.

"You're not the Mouse." *"Toowhoo, not I,*
But he's somewhere nearby, eating gruffalo pie."

The snow fell fast and the wind blew wild.
"I'm not scared," said the Gruffalo's Child.

Aha! Oho! A track in the snow!
Whose is this track and where does it go?
Whiskers at last! And an underground house!
Could this be the home of the Big Bad Mouse?

Out slunk the creature. His eyes weren't fiery.
His tail wasn't scaly. His whiskers weren't wiry.

"You're not the Mouse."   *"Oh no, not me.*
He's under a tree – drinking gruffalo tea."

"It's all a trick!" said the Gruffalo's Child
As she sat on a stump where the snow lay piled.
"I don't *believe* in the Big Bad Mouse . . .

"But here comes a little one, out of his house!
Not big, not bad, but a mouse at least –
You'll taste good as a midnight feast."

"Wait!" said the mouse. "Before you eat,
There's a friend of mine that you ought to meet.
If you'll let me hop onto a hazel twig
I'll beckon my friend so bad and big."

The Gruffalo's Child unclenched her fist.
"The Big Bad Mouse – so he *does* exist!"
The mouse hopped into the hazel tree.
He beckoned, then said, *"Just wait and see."*

Out came the moon. It was bright and round.
A terrible shadow fell onto the ground.

Who is this creature so big, bad and strong?
His tail and his whiskers are terribly long.
His ears are enormous, and over his shoulder
He carries a nut as big as a boulder!

"The Big Bad Mouse!" yelled the Gruffalo's Child.
The mouse jumped down from the twig and smiled.

Aha! Oho! Prints in the snow.
Whose are these footprints? Where do they go?

The footprints led to the gruffalo cave

Where the Gruffalo's Child was a bit less brave.

The Gruffalo's Child was a bit less bored . . .

And the Gruffalo snored
and snored and snored.

Aha! Oho! Prints in the snow.

Can you follow each trail of footprints with your finger
to find out who it belongs to?

Have fun moving like the creatures in the snowy wood.
You could try flying like the owl, sliding along like
the snake, or slinking about like the fox on four legs.

Or try to tiptoe like
the Gruffalo's Child

Try using a different voice for the narrator and for each character as you sing the song

The Gruffalo's Child Song

 Where are you going to, Gruffalo's Child,
All by yourself through the woods so wild?

 Aha! Oho! To look for the Big Bad Mouse.
Where can he be? I'll ask the Snake.

 He's down by the lake, eating Gruffalo cake.
Aha! Oho! Beware of the Big Bad Mouse.

 Where can he be? Will Owl tell me?

 He's under a tree, drinking Gruffalo tea.
Too-whit! Too-whoo! Beware of the Big Bad Mouse.

 Where can he be? The Fox looks sly:

 He's somewhere nearby, eating Gruffalo pie.
Aha! Oho! Beware of the Big Bad Mouse.

 Who is this creature so big and strong?
His tail and his whiskers are terribly long.
Oh help! Oh no! It must be the Big Bad Mouse!

 Where are you going to, Gruffalo's Child,
All by yourself through the woods so wild?

 Away! Back home! To hide from the Big Bad Mouse.

Visit Gruffalo.com/songs to watch a video of Julia singing this song

Writing The Gruffalo's Child

I had such fun writing *The Gruffalo's Child*. I wanted to write a follow-up book to *The Gruffalo*, and I liked the idea of turning the original story on its head and having the predators trick a gruffalo, but still keeping the mouse as the main trickster.

I thought about what new trick the mouse might play, and that's when I came up with the idea of the Big Bad Mouse shadow. But then I started to worry. The forest floor in the deep dark wood is usually covered in earth and leaves and twigs, so perhaps a shadow wouldn't show up clearly. That's what made me think of setting the story in the winter, because snow on the ground would give a nice clear shadow.

This led me to think about tracks in the snow. I love nature and often go for walks on the South Downs near my house, but I'm not great at identifying animal tracks. In the winter, I've seen the tracks of dogs, foxes and birds in the snow, but never a snake track. Then Axel pointed out that snakes hibernate in winter. And that's when I learned what track a snake makes in the snow . . . none! They're not awake to make any.

But I really wanted to include all the same animals from the original story, so I decided that this is a special picture book snake who helpfully stays awake in order to trick the Gruffalo's Child. Then Axel made me laugh because in the pictures he drew the snake looking very sleepy. Take a look and see.

Now the book is 15 years old. Happy birthday to the mouse, fox, owl, sleepy snake, Gruffalo, and of course, to his daughter – the Gruffalo's Child!

Julia Donaldson

The Gruffalo's Child has been translated into over 50 languages!

It has been enjoyed by millions of children around the world

Drawing The Gruffalo's Child

What would a gruffalo look like as a child? I wondered about this when I first read Julia's story.

Would the Gruffalo's Child have a poisonous wart like her dad? I decided that she'd have to be a bit older for a wart, and also for knobbly knees. What about horns? I made them smaller and rounder on the Gruffalo's Child. There are a few other differences too. You can see that her eyes are yellow instead of orange.

When I first drew the Gruffalo's Child, she looked quite different. She didn't have any prickles and she was the same colour as her dad. But then I gave her pink prickles and made her a different shade of brown with a white tummy. Now I can't imagine her any other way.

At first, I thought the snowy wood at night might be hard to draw and to paint. In fact, the trickiest thing was the shadow of the Big Bad Mouse in the snow – but it looks real enough to scare a gruffalo.

Happy birthday, Gruffalo's Child!

Axel Scheffler

The Gruffalo's Child also stars in a film and a stage show

Gruffalo's Child play scene

Setting up

Look inside the jacket of your book and you'll find your snowy play scene. Stand the play scene on a flat surface, such as a table or the floor. Next, carefully press out the characters at the back of the book. To make the characters stand up, fold back the base at the bottom.

Time to play

Now it's time to play! You could use your characters to act out the story. Look at the pictures in the book to help you remember what happens. Or ask a grown-up to read the story aloud while you act it out with your press-out characters.

The mouse's shadow

Making the mouse's shadow can be lots of fun. Why not try using a torch as the moon to make the shadow? Dim the lights and shine the torch behind your press-out mouse so you see its shadow on the ground. You'll need to work out the best place to hold the torch to make a really big shadow.

Or you could draw the mouse's shadow on a piece of paper and put it on the ground. How about tracing this shadow from the book?

Putting on a show

Would you like to use your play scene and press-out characters to put on a puppet show of *The Gruffalo's Child* for your family and friends? You'll need to practise the show first before you put it on for an audience.

Why not ask your friends to put on the show with you? Choose who will play each character and have fun trying out different voices. The Gruffalo probably has a deep voice, and Mouse might have a squeaky voice. But what do you think the Gruffalo's Child sounds like?

Here's another idea – why not sing The Gruffalo's Child Song as part of your show? You could sing it at the end for a grand finale and ask your audience to join in!

Making up stories

You could even make up your own stories with your snowy play scene and press-out characters. For instance, what would happen if the Gruffalo woke up from his sleep and saw the mouse? Have fun thinking up your own ideas!

Keep your press-out characters in an envelope or a box so they don't get lost. Then you can use them again and again!

Can you spot Mouse's house in your play scene?

What else can you see?